First published in 2015 by Rockpool Children's Books Ltd.

This edition published in 2015 by Rockpool Children's Books Ltd.

Published in association with Albury Books.
Albury Court, Albury, Thame
OX9 2LP, United Kingdom

www.AlburyBooks.com

For orders: Kuperard Publishers and Distributors
+44 (0) 208 4462440

Text and Illustrations copyright © Stuart Trotter 2015

Stuart Trotter has asserted the moral rights
to be identified as the author and illustrator of this book.
© Rockpool Children's Books Ltd. 2015

Printed and bound in China

ISBN 978-1-906081-91-1 (Paperback)

rockpool
children's books

Stuart Trotter

Polar White

and the
"Woo hoo" day

On board were
Polar White's jungle friends.

It was their winter holiday!

They were all very excited and looking forward to their snowy adventures!

"**Woo hoo**" they shouted.

Polar White, and little Ted,
sledged down the hill to meet them.

"**Woo hoo**" they whooped.

They all climbed on board
a cable car to take them
to the mountaintops.

"Here we go!" they cried.
But they were just too heavy,
and the cable car couldn't move!

"Oh dear," thought Polar White.
"I must sort this out."
So he called...

...**Pete the pilot**,
who roared to the rescue
with his helicopter!

"Hang on!"
he yelled,

and with a lot of huff,
and quite a bit of puff,
he whisked the stranded chums
into the air!

**"Woo
hoo"**
they yelped.

After a whizzing, whirling, rip roaring ride, and lots of "whoops" and "Woo hoo's", Pete lowered them gently on to the mountaintop.

Wally Wolf was planning
something very naughty.
Just as the chums
were fixing their
skis and snowboards,
he called...

"Boo!"

very loudly across the valley.
The echoing sound caused
a small avalanche!

All the snow rushed down
the mountainside.
Thank goodness the animals had their
skis and snowboards – they scooted
down safely, yelling,

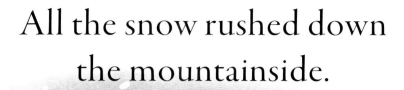

"Woo
hoo"

as they went.

But at the bottom,
Elephant got stuck fast in the snow!
"Oops!" said Elephant.

"Don't worry," said Polar White.
"We'll soon get you out of there."
So he called...

...Steve the snow blower!
With his new portable snow blower,
Steve sucked all the snow off Elephant
and dumped it on Wally Wolf,
who'd come to see how much
trouble he'd caused.

"Waaaargh!"
yelled Wally.

But soon there was another crisis.

"Help!"

shouted the little monkeys.
They'd been swept by the snow
onto a high craggy peak.
Charlie Chimp quickly
climbed the rock face to the rescue.
"Wow!" gasped Polar White.

With the monkeys clinging on,
Charlie para-glided down the slope...
and off the mountain.

"Woo hoo"

shouted the little
monkeys excitedly.
"See you all at Polar White's
for hot chocolate,"
called Charlie.

"Woo hoo"

they whooped again.

Remembering to dig out
Wally Wolf first, who said,
"Sorry, everyone,"
they all skied down the slopes to
Polar White's to drink
hot chocolate by a roaring fire.
"Another great holiday
with Polar White!"
said Jimmy Giraffe.

"Woo hoo"

chorused
the jungle
chums!